Riff-Raff Rabbit

by ALISON RITCHIE

and illustrated by PAUL CHERRILL

Blue Bananas

For T.G.

A.R.

For Mum, Dad and Chris

P.C.

Riff-Raff Rabbit played the drums.

He had his own band.

There was Syd

the snake on

saxophone

and Hot Dog on trombone.

Fat Cat played
double bass

and Fingers
Racoon played
the spoons.

9

Their biggest fan was Riff-Raff's little brother, Ronald. He thought they were the greatest.

Mr and Mrs Riff-Raff did not think the
Raging Riff-Raffs were the greatest.
Mr and Mrs Riff-Raff thought they were
one big horrible noise.

When the
Raging
Riff-Raffs
practised
in Riff-Raff's
bedroom,
Mr Riff-Raff
banged
on the wall
with a rolled-up
newspaper.

When they practised in the
bathroom, Mrs Riff-Raff
banged on the door
with her hair-
brush.

13

When they practised in the back garden,

the neighbours threw water over the fence.

But that didn't stop the Raging Riff-Raffs.

They just kept on playing.

They played
in the kitchen,

the sitting room

and the hall.

They played

in the shed

and the

greenhouse.

Mr and Mrs Riff-Raff couldn't stand it any longer. Mr Riff-Raff was tearing his hair out.

They took Riff-Raff's drums away. They banned the members of the Raging Riff-Raffs. 'Go home and don't come back!' they said.

Out went Syd on saxophone and Hot Dog on trombone.

Out went Fat Cat on double bass

and Fingers Racoon on spoons.

21

Riff-Raff didn't know what to do.

He mooched.

He moped.

He wouldn't eat.

He couldn't sleep.

But the next day, Riff-Raff played . . .

the dustbins, the saucepans and the car

bonnet.

He played the television,

the goldfish bowl . . .

. . . and Ronald.

Mr and Mrs Riff-Raff couldn't stand it any longer. 'OK, Riff-Raff, you win! We give in! We'll find somewhere else for the Raging Riff-Raffs to play.'

29

All through
the night,
Mr and Mrs
Riff-Raff dug
a sound-proof
burrow, deep
underground.
It was a
special place
where Riff-Raff
could be as noisy
as he liked, and
no one would
hear a thing.

33

'OK, Riff-Raff,' said Mrs Riff-Raff

the next morning, 'this is YOUR place.'

'And it's the ONLY place where you

can play!' added Mr Riff-Raff.

Riff-Raff hung up
a sign outside.

He phoned the
members of the band.

That afternoon . . .

Back came Syd on saxophone

and Hot Dog on trombone.

36

Back came Fat Cat on double bass

and Fingers Racoon on spoons.

The Raging Riff-Raffs were together

again!

They could play and play and play!

Morning,

noon

and night,

the ground sh**oo**k,
rattled,
and rolled.

But Mr and Mrs Riff-Raff could not hear a sound.

They were very happy.

Ronald was *not* happy.

He mooched.

He moped.

He wouldn't eat.

He couldn't sleep.

But the next day . . .